RICK
THE DOG WITH A
Difference

igloobooks

Fetch is so often a dog's
favourite game,
but Rick has just never
quite felt the same.

When he's at the park
and his pals chase a stick...

... they're all too busy
to play with poor Rick.

He played as a pup and was quick as a flash.
But the game ended up in a big puppy...

... CRASH!

When Rick
tried again...

... the stick fell
on the floor.

He thought he
was done...

... but they kept
throwing more.

One day, he meets Duck who thinks swimming's too soggy.

"You don't need sticks to be a good doggy.

"I have some great friends you really should meet."

So, they go to see Mouse who lives down the street.

Mouse says hello and he squeaks with a grin,
"I'm *not* like other mice. Shall I begin?

Although I love dairy,
I'm *not* allowed cheese.

Just one tiny nibble
makes me cough and wheeze."

Next, Owl swoops over. Though most fly at night,

HOO-HOO,

he hoots,

"Flying's great
when it's light."

Cow was so bored with the grass she once chewed.
She MOO-MOOS and says, "Now I eat tasty food."

Rick starts to see there's
no need to like sticks.
It's not a problem
that he needs to fix.

Then the friends share a picnic.
It's all dairy-free.
And Cow brings some treats
for posh afternoon tea.

When everyone's full up
with sweet, scrummy cake,
Duck takes his little boat
down to the lake.

He says it's the only way he likes to float.
Cat MEOWS and asks, "Can I ride on your boat?"

Cat wants
to play, but her
friends are all snoring.

"They love it," she sighs.
"But sleep is so boring!"

"It's okay," says Rick.
"Don't feel like you're wrong.
Differences make
everyone get along."

"Hooray!" yells Cat,
with one great big leap.
"Playing's much more
fun than going to sleep."

Rick has an idea and says, "Let's have a race.
I want to play something that's *not* fetch or chase!"

The games
are so good,
lots more dogs
join in, too.

WOOF!
"We're so glad
we can all play
with you."

Now, everyone can play all day with Rick...

... who never again will chase after a stick.